I0624408

Tales from the Canyons of the Damned

DANIEL ARTHUR SMITH

Tales from the Canyons of the Damned No. 1

Copyright © 2015 Daniel Arthur Smith

ISBN-13: 978-0692572863
ISBN-10:0692572864

Edited By
Crystal Watanabe

Cover By
Daniel Arthur Smith

Also Written by Daniel Arthur Smith

The Cameron Kincaid Adventures
The Cathari Treasure
The Somali Deception

Literary Fiction
The Potter's Daughter
Opening Day: A Short Story

Horror Fiction
Agroland
Tower

Science Fiction
Hugh Howey Lives

~*~

For Susan, Tristan, & Oliver, as all things are.

~*~

Sandhogs

Six hundred feet beneath the gray streets of midtown Manhattan, below the parking garages, the basements and subbasements, far deeper than the winding nests of electric conduits and gas lines, a tiny electric bulb slowly came to life with a dull honey glow, three feet above the head of Jed McGuire. The small bulb appeared to float, the wire it dangled from hidden in the too thick mist.

The blow-pipes were deafening. That's what he figured was producing all of the mist– the moisture, the heat. They'd blasted air and water into the tube for hours, and in those hours, Jed's vision was knocked out. Not only him, all of the guys.

Jed squinted to gain focus. Yes, the cavern was mistier than he'd seen it in fifteen years as a sandhog. But he was seeing again. Glowing halos hovered around him and below each, larger glossed beacons began to appear. The other sandhogs were turning on their flashlights. Below the dim bulb, he could make out the top of the hospital stretcher propped against a wall. He had his bearings, his location. He was in the middle of the deep tunnel, a tight twelve-foot circle of cave that ran a hundred yards to either side from where he stood.

And it was hot. It had been hot since the lights went out, since everything went black. The humid mist had brought the temperature up from the usual seventy degrees. Way up.

Something had gone wrong. Jed couldn't fathom what.

1

There hadn't been an explosion. No charges were set.

Only the instant blackness – the lights had gone out.

The radios worked on their end, but no one answered on the other.

Jimmy had made his way to the cage. The call buzzer didn't sound. They all made their way around all right, even without sight. They were sandhogs, the six of them, all third generation. Except Jonesy, he was second.

But there was no doubt in their minds that they were alone down there in the hidden caverns beneath the deepest, darkest, dankest, section of the city. No doubt, that is, until Lenny screamed, "Get it off me! Get it off me!"

The other five men circled around the shaking lights. Up close, they could see the terror on the man's aged face. A tough man, a large man, a man that could hold a jumping jackleg straight into a wall while the hammer was at full bore, without flinching.

And he was screaming a wretched painful torrent of a scream. A scream that bounced and echoed and returned to their ears with cutting force.

"What is it?" Cal asked as he and the others washed their lights across Lenny's bulk of a chest. Nothing on his dirt-covered Carhart seemed flawed, no tears.

"Down there!" he screamed again. "Down there! Get it off me!" hopping to the side until he fell upon a buttress.

That was when Jed saw Lenny's foot, the thing on Lenny's foot, the purple and crimson streaked gelatin mass that oozed around the stump where the boot had been, where the toes had been, the thing sucking up the canvas of his leg.

"What the hell is that?" Jimmy yelled.

"Shit," Jonesy chimed.

"Aarrgh!" Lenny yelled, no longer making words.

The steam from the jelly was thicker than the mist, and the smell was acrid, rancid.

"What do we do?" Markie asked.

"I dunno," Cal said. "I think he's goin' into shock."

"Cut it off 'em," Jed said.

"What?" Jimmy asked.

"Cut it off!" Jed yelled.

"Yeah," Cal said, "get the med kit."

Lenny's scream had turned into a constant loud agonizing moan.

"Shit," Jonesy said again. "We're gonna help you, Len. We're gonna help."

Markie drug the plastic case close —but not too close— to Lenny's leg then opened it wide so they all could see.

"Okay," he asked. "What now?"

Jed pointed his finger toward the kit and then jerked it half back. "That bottle there," he said, "that's rubbing alcohol. Pour it on."

Markie pushed the case toward Jed. "I'm not touchen' it."

Cal swiftly dropped to one knee, swiped the bottle from the side of the case, twisted the cap, and tossed it away. "Here goes," he said, and began to pour the clear liquid across Lenny's shin where the purplish jelly burned against the flesh and frayed canvas pants.

Lenny let out a deafening howl that brought Cal's free hand up to his ear, causing him to cast his weight closer to the goo. The hand that held the bottle dropped nearer, almost touching the mass. Only a flinch, a shift for a second coinciding with the yell, the reaction to the pain, and that's all it took, a second, and in that second, Cal realized, Jed realized, whomever else in the group who was watching realized, that the gelatin mass on Lenny's foot was not some chemical mass he'd stepped in, was not some spill or compound. No, the blob was organic, and the blob was alive, and this they saw when the blood crimson-streaked creature lashed out with a protruding bit of translucent matter, latched onto Cal's fingers, and then sucked itself up onto his hand.

Lenny's horrendous roar had fallen to a whimper. But Cal wasn't paying attention to him anymore, and neither was Jed or any of the others. Cal was being tugged, a kitten caught on a string, he couldn't shake the thick purple jelly loose.

"It's glued to me," Cal said.

The others said nothing. There was nothing to be said. It was glue and behaved the same. The more Cal twitched, the further he entangled his hand.

Jed saw the worry in Cal's tightened face.

"It burns," Cal said with a flick of his wrists, and then the surprise, when the jelly surged up toward his forearm. "Ah!" Cal yelled.

"Shit," Jimmy said. "That thing is growing."

And Jed could see that thing was growing. The mass hadn't displaced onto Cal, rather had grown onto him, and was constricting, pulling Cal's arm in, in toward Lenny's leg.

Jed slipped from his moment of stupor. "Let's pull them apart."

"What?" Jimmy asked.

"Grab Lenny. I'll grab Cal. Markie, help him out."

Jed hunched over behind Cal, slipped his arms beneath his shoulders, and with a hefty thrust attempted to lift him away from Lenny.

"It's no use," Cal said between gritted teeth.

He was right. The two didn't separate. The mass appeared to fight the attempt, to pull them closer, tighter.

"Hell!" Jonesy yelled.

The others' eyes darted to Jonesy and with them their headlamps. Lenny had kicked his foot up, the goo-covered foot, and caught Jonesy on the calf.

"How'd that happen?" Jimmy asked.

"Get your pants off," Cal said, in pain, yet still in charge. "Quick!"

Jonesy fumbled to unzip his Carhart jacket and the vest beneath to reach his belt. He slid the leather from the buckle, ripped at the button of the Levis, tucked his thumbs into his waists, and pushed down his pants. They were as far as his knees before he yelped and bucked forward, falling over onto Lenny's leg, Cal's arm, and the crimson purple jelly goo.

Jed propped his back against a four-hundred-million-year-old chunk of black schist. The sparkles that reflected from the rock were the same as those in his eyes.

There was nothing to say.

Jimmy and Markie's lights became foggy glows as they eased away from the three knotted men on the floor. Lenny had stopped making sounds, Cal was moaning, and Jonesy was convulsing, just a little, but vibrating just the same, as if there were something in him, and there was, something hungry, something growing.

Jed watched until he couldn't. He watched the jelly bubble through the back of Jonesy's canvas jacket. He didn't want to see the blob dissolve his friends altogether, so he climbed up and made his way further into the cave, and then rested just far enough away that he could still see everyone's lamps through the fog.

Until one by one, their lamps went out.

~*~

The Penthouse

The K-cups that Jack remembered seeing in the drawer were gone. That girl he was dating, Jan, must have drunk them. He didn't remember the last time he used the countertop *one-cup-atta-time* Keurig. Breakfast usually meant a coffee on the street. But no power for another day meant no elevators, thus no coffee. But all was not lost. There were two bottles of scotch on the counter and a bottle of Drambuie. He opened the bottom freezer drawer of the Sub-Zero and knuckled into the ice bin. Though the bottom was a puddle, there were still a ton of cubes left. Jack cinched the sash of his lucky red robe and did the only thing a man could do alone in the penthouse of his glass-towered building. One Rusty Nail coming up.

He tossed two cubes in a rock glass, topped them with the scotch, and the filled the rest of the glass with the Drambuie. All he needed was a lemon, a little tart to curb the honey heather sweet of the Drambuie. He opened the dark empty fridge, already stale without the coolness to mask the odor. There was food inside, no lemons or limes, all sauces, spreads, and condiments. The pantry wasn't looking much better. His diet was take-out. The only thing on the shelves were almonds, cookies, cheese puffs, and pretzels. There was a box of German chocolate cake mix in the back, and a container of frosting to the side. Jan must've bought it. And it wasn't of much use. Short of eggs and oil the mix was just powder.

None of that sounded appetizing, except for that fresh

Rusty Nail.

The refrigerator was not totally empty. The door was lined with two kinds of BBQ sauce, Worcestershire, A1, Dijon, a green bottle of lite soy, a short jar of maraschino cherries, and yes, to the rescue, the plastic lemon. Just as good, the same thing as far as the scotch and Jack were concerned. He grabbed the plastic lemon from the fridge door and shook it near his ear – empty, a lemon of a lemon. He flung the empty plastic into the dark recess of the top shelf and swiped the maraschino cherries from the door. The cherries weren't tart, but you work with what you got.

He had to exert a couple of waist-level thrusts onto the lid before he heard the *POP* release, and then he was a go.

By the stem a cherry for him, two cherries for the glass, and… Why not? A dash of juice too, and voila, a Bloody Nail. Not exactly, it was cherry juice, not cherry brandy, but you work with what you got. A sip of the cocktail… and… Jack swished the sweet liquor through the front of his mouth, and then swallowed. "Aah," he said. "Not bad at all."

He reached for the fridge handle with his pinky, caught himself, and then set the cherry jar on the counter next to the booze. The temperature was about the same inside as out.

The small kitchen was the only shadowy spot in the penthouse and thus depressing, so Jack slipped his hand into the pocket of his lucky red robe and strolled across the chocolate board flooring to the milk-white glass wall.

Cocktail — scratch that, Bloody Nail — in hand, leisurely day, as good as it gets. Jack sucked a deep breath in through his nose and then let it out. A drink. If things were so great, why then… He leaned close to the glass to see if he could catch a glimpse of the street, or even the apartment below. Nothing. The fog was so thick. The outside of his apartment could have been white smoke, white steam, whatever the difference, it didn't matter.

He paced toward the glass coffee table. Gazed at the brown leather loveseat and the matching sofa. He had only sat on the loveseat twice. Once when he purchased it, and then once after it was delivered. Jack stared at it for a moment — another sweet pull, another swish — and then decided to sit down on the chocolate leather.

So he did.

Right in the center. And the leather was nice, sucked him in. He raised his brow, satisfied, and ran his left hand across the top of the leather. He wondered for a moment what kind of leather it was. It hadn't occurred to him before. The salesman in Soho had said Italian leather and then charged four thousand for the sofa and two thousand for the loveseat. But what did that mean, Italian leather. He had assumed bovine. Cow leather. He pivoted his head to the right to meet the rock glass raising in his hand, and that was when he saw it, from his peripheral, out the windowed wall. A few feet, maybe a yard or two away. There had been a red flash.

Had there been?

Jack's neck crooked forward. Alert, watching.

Nothing.

The muscles near his spine relaxed and he finished his attempt at taking a drink.

"Whoa," he said aloud, because he saw it again. Directly in front of where he sat. There was no doubt this time. Something red was out there. And it hadn't passed by his apartment, flown by. Whatever that red blur was, out there in the fog, just beyond his view, it was hovering. The glimpse he caught was thin, horizontal, not a bird, but not a balloon, at least not a round balloon. Jack shuffled his shoulder blades into the back cushion. Finally, some entertainment.

Jack didn't have to wait long. The red line zinged by again. This time he noticed though, that whatever the red thing was, it was long. Because his gaze was set on a small foot-and-a-half wide window in the fog, and he could see – the tube – sliding left. So it was a long red tube, and real long, because it slid past through that little hole in the fog for a good forty-five seconds before disappearing again. He did the math, sort of, a couple of feet going by per second would be… Jack tilted head to the side and saluted the outside vapor with his rock glass.

He waited for his gleaming red friend to reappear, either in a glimpse or at length, but the long tube did not return.

Jack rose from the loveseat, circled the glass-topped teak coffee table, and approached the transparent wall.

Nothing.

He peered deeply into the glowing white void, the creamy swirl of endless vapor. Whatever he saw out there in the mist, as long and large as it was, had passed.

And so had most of his Bloody Nail.

Jack shook the cocktail to knock the cubes together, a subconscious attempt to leach the last of the booze from the ice. And then he pivoted toward the interior of the apartment and raised the drink high to swill down the remainder.

Jack may not have seen anything out into the beyond. But something saw him. And while the last of the sweet Maraschino Drambuie scotch concoction drizzled onto his tongue, the long tube that was not a tube returned, unfurling, reaching, lashing for Jack.

He did not see the massive tentacle hurl into the transparent wall a foot to his back, nor did he see the thick glass shatter to shards.

It was the wall that saved him from the blow, forcing him onto the chocolate board flooring. It was the loveseat that was his demise. Because when that long gleaming red arm swung into the hollow of Jack's penthouse to search for him, it found the small sofa instead, and dragged the two thousand dollar Italian leather piece right out into the abyss.

And Jack, because he was between that piece of furniture and the outside nothing, peeled away from his penthouse as well.

~*~

The Harbor

Madison had been standing outside of the bathroom door for an eternal ten minutes. Ten minutes becomes an eternity when you're in the middle of the New York Harbor, everyone is staring at you, and your eleven-month old is wailing. Little Miranda had broken down on deck, her diaper diarrhea-soaked. The trip to New York wasn't agreeing with her. The trip to the Big Apple wasn't agreeing with Mommy too much either. But if you lived up in Red Wing Minnesota opportunities to travel to New York City didn't come along every day.

Since the baby arrived, she hadn't even made her way up to Minneapolis. Madison hadn't really gone anywhere. So when Todd told her he could bring her along on a five-day trip, she thought she was dreaming. She called Peggy, and Leslie, and of course she had called her sister Fran, not to gloat necessarily, that would have been rude. But to let them know Todd was doing really well. So well that his company was sending him to Manhattan, and he was bringing her along. She had the trip all planned out. She was going to go to all of the places she saw on Sex and the City — it was absolutely one of her favorite shows, she had even named little Miranda after one of the characters. She was going to take the three-hour Sex and the City tour and go to Magnolia Bakery and indulge on one of those famous cupcakes Carrie always ate when she was gossiping with Miranda, visit the site of Carrie and Big's wedding rehearsal dinner, have a Cosmo at MePa. She had Cosmos back in Red Wing, but the idea of a Cosmo at MePa tickled her. She was even going to go to that naughty sex shop over on seventh, the Pleasure Chest, where Charlotte bought her *Rabbit*.

Except the trip hadn't gone the way she had planned at all, at least not yet.

Todd had spent the last few days working from morning til night. She had only seen the hotel and the hotel restaurant. And the Holiday Inn Four Seasons wasn't as fancy as she'd imagined it to be, neither was the neighborhood. She had taken Miranda out one day to buy diapers and formula. She saw three homeless people all on the same block. And everything in New York looked like it needed to be scrubbed. The place was dirty. Especially this ferry, this ferry that she didn't want to be on in the first place. Todd finally had some time to spend with her and this was where they ended up. Them and a man named Terry. Terry seemed like a nice man. He was from New Jersey. Terry wasn't married. Madison thought that a man Terry's age should be, he was almost thirty. It was Terry's idea to go out on the ferry. "It's the best way to see the statue and the skyline." That's what Terry had said. "The Circle Line will just cost you money. You don't want to do anything so touristy." He had said that too. But she did want to do something touristy. She didn't want to be standing outside of this bathroom on this filthy deck while Miranda was crying her eyes out. Poor baby.

Madison bobbed Miranda up and down and softly whispered, "It's okay, it's okay," over and over into the baby's ear. She brushed her face up against the little girl's tear-soaked cheeks. The little sign near the handle was still red, no vacancy. She leaned Miranda into her shoulder and then raised her other arm to knock on the door, and then, with a second thought, reached for the handle. Her finger had almost taken hold when, with two fast clicks of the latch, the door swung inward.

Madison eased back and lifted her hand to Miranda's head.

The woman that stepped into the doorframe was rough to

Madison's taste, certainly not a Midwestern girl. She was wearing a short denim skirt, a bright yellow tee — she'd had the collar and sleeves removed, roughly by scissors from the look — and was revealing way more cleavage than any decent woman should. And the good lord had endowed this girl. The woman's blonde hair was teased high, or rather brunette with a ton of blonde accents. And the tattoo, some kind of crazy black snake or dragon curling up her arm. Carrie might have called her a hot mess.

The woman's eyes went wide at Madison, and she sucked in a long breath through her nose. "If you want a tampon," the woman said, "the machine's empty."

Madison felt the corner of her mouth begin to curl up. What a disgusting thing to say. No one in Minnesota would ever say such a thing. Miranda squealed. Madison closed her eyes and waited for the excuse of a woman to pass. She opened her eyes and then stepped into the filthy Lysol-smelling closet of a bathroom to change her daughter's diarrhea filled diaper.

Madison looked at the warped reflection of her and her little girl in the tin metal mirror. She didn't want to be in New York City anymore. She wanted to go back to Red Wing. She thought she might cry, and she might have, except Miranda beat her to it. Again she whispered into her daughter's ear to soothe her.

The light flickered and the little closet of a bathroom went dark.

"What now?" she asked aloud.

She continued to bob Miranda up and down. She just wanted to get a fresh diaper on the child and get her back on deck with Todd and that man Terry. She could feed her baby up there and everything could be fine.

Then that loud hum, the roar that had been a constant since they had left the pier, ceased. The diesel engines had stopped.

Miranda stopped crying as well.

Silence.

The room was black, but at least there was peace.

And then, from out on deck, Madison heard the first of the

screams. There was one, and then two, and then too many to count, all chiming in a horrific harmony. She fumbled for the doorknob, the latch, the handle, but it was black, and she couldn't see where it was. She found the flat of the door with her hand, ran her fingers to the frame, and then started down the side. She found the handle and was about to push down to release the lock when the world jolted forward.

Madison flew to the front of the small space, slamming her body against the child's and the wall, the wall that seemed to be at an angle. But she couldn't tell, it was dark, it was black. People were screaming, all around people were screaming, and there was a new sound, the sound of bending, twisting metal, twisting, crushing metal.

Madison rolled to her side. Miranda was screaming now too, so much noise in that small space. She frantically searched for the latch again, now above her as she lay flat on the wall, on her back. She found the latch. She pushed the latch down. And through the freed door burst in — along with more blackness — the so cold harbor water.

~*~

The moss and seaweed-covered rocks were slimy and foul, but they were warm, so much warmer than the harbor and the river had been. Her arms ached, her legs ached, her ribs, her chest, her neck, it all ached, too much for her to pull herself up out of the water and onto the esplanade. When the harbor engulfed her, when the world went black, when the ferry and the harbor both tried to pull her down, when that donut of a preserver slipped onto her leg, she'd squeezed it tighter than any man she had ever held there. Unable to see, she wrapped her arms around another floating cushion when she bobbed to the surface. And she rode the current, rode the cold water tide out and back in. She held tight in only her short denim skirt and sleeveless yellow tee, too numb to shiver, too angry to let go. And when the current washed Rosalee up against the slime covered stone of the Battery, she blindly curled into their stony warm womb. And then she slept or passed out, and that didn't matter, because she'd lived through whatever happened out on the harbor, through whatever happened to that ferry.

When she opened her eyes, she gazed up from the rocks to the long pier, the long building and clock tower with the words Pier A printed across the bottom. Rosalee recognized the building. The building was across Battery Park from the Staten Island Ferry terminal.

Hours passed by and she did not move. She just stared, stared at the clock tower.

Beyond the clock was a mist, no… a fog. A thick cloud that hovered and danced behind the tower.

She may have not moved at all. She may have stayed there on the rocks. The huge round stones were warm, and the large drops plopping onto her forehead, arms, legs, and hair were warm, everything was warm. The light of day was fading and Rosalee, her body in so much pain, was about to drift off again, to close her eyes one more time.

The tide changed all of that. The first small icy wave to ripple against her aching feet, that was all it took. All it took to invigorate Rosalee, to remind her who she was.

"Oh, hell," she said aloud. She pushed herself up onto her hands, the burn of ache punishing her as she did. "Girl, you gotta move your ass."

Once she found her footing she carefully maneuvered to the break wall, wiped her hands against the concrete and then against the denim of her skirt. A glance down told her that the tee was ripped and that she was wearing no bra was no secret to the world. She was barely covered at all anymore.

"Oh, hell," she said again. "Barefoot and bare assed. Ain't that wonderful."

~*~

~*~

THE
END

~*~

.

ABOUT THE AUTHOR

Daniel Arthur Smith is the author of the international bestsellers **HUGH HOWEY LIVES, THE CATHARI TREASURE, THE SOMALI DECEPTION**, and a few other novels and short stories.

He was raised in Michigan and graduated from Western Michigan University where he studied philosophy, with focus on cognitive science, meta-physics, and comparative religion. He began his career as a bartender, barista, poetry house proprietor, teacher, and then became a technologist and futurist for the Fortune 100 across the Americas and Europe.

Daniel has traveled to over 300 cities in 22 countries, residing in Los Angeles, Kalamazoo, Prague, Crete, and now writes in Manhattan where he lives with his wife and young sons.

For more information, visit danielarthursmith.com

~*~